GirlfriendZ

Music is NOT banned!

GirlFriendZ
Sing a Song of Sixpence
by Roger Hurn
Illustrated by Kenny Kiernan

Published by Ransom Publishing Ltd.
Radley House, 8 St. Cross Road, Winchester, Hampshire
SO23 9HX, UK
www.ransom.co.uk

ISBN   978 178127 155 1
First published in 2013

Sing a Song of Sixpence

Roger Hurn

Illustrated by Kenny Kiernan

Ransom

Kelly Montez

Like · Comment · Friend

Hey, I'm Kelly Montez, and unless you've been living in a cave for the past year you'll know I'm in the band *GirlFriendZ*.

Yeah, that's right, I'm the one with the killer looks and a voice like gravel dipped in honey. And *GirlFriendZ* is the number one band in the world – or it *was*, until the day the aliens invaded Earth and banned music! Those creepoids are *so* not cool.

But don't worry guys, we're not going to let them get away with that. *GirlFriendZ* will carry on making music and there's no way a bunch of alien weirdos in MIB (Music is Banned) is going to stop us!

Yaz Jackson

Like · Comment · Friend

Hiya guys, Yaz here. I was born in a circus and my mum and dad were acrobats, so that's why I'm always doing somersaults, cartwheels and back flips on stage. On our next tour I'm gonna walk across the stage on a high wire! How cool is that?

Yeah, you did hear me right. There WILL be another *GirlFriendZ* tour – just as soon as we find a way to send the Zargons back to their home planet with their creepy alien tails between their legs.

Olivia Parsons

Like · Comment · Friend

Hi *GirlFriendZ* fans. My name is Olivia – but everyone calls me Liv. I know I look like the girl next door, but I can be a bit of a wild child when it comes to music! I just love getting up on stage and singing my heart out!

But now those freaky aliens are arresting musicians and destroying all the musical instruments they can get their tentacles on! It makes me so mad, but they'll never catch us and stop us singing.

That's a promise!

Eve Rossi

Like · Comment · Friend

Hello everybody. I'm Eve, the girl with the crazy hair and the personality to match!

It's great being in *GirlFriendZ* 'cos it gives me the chance to wear all kinds of amazing outfits. I love designing my own clothes and it gives me a buzz when I see you guys copying my look!

I know the Zargons are trying to stop us having fun – but don't fret guys, we are *so* gonna have the last laugh!

Charlotte Opirah

Like · Comment · Friend

OK, it's me, Charlotte. Usually I'd rather sing than talk, 'cos I'm the best singer in the band. Hey, just kidding!!

But I've got something to say that can't be put into a song. It's this. We absolutely *have* to find a way to beat the Zargons! They must have a weakness – and I've got a suspicion it has something to do with music.

Think about it guys. They have banned music and they're doing some kind of alien mind-wipe, so musicians and singers forget how to play and sing. Why? Well, I'm gonna make it my business to find out!

8

Finn the roadie

Like · Comment · Friend

Hey, I'm Finn and I have the best job in the world. I'm the *roadie* (that's road manager) for *GirlFriendZ*. Well, it *was* the best job until the Zargons arrived and we had to go on the run. Now my job is about getting the girls to their secret gigs *and* keeping them out of the Zargon's clutches! You see, the Zargon agents of MIB track down musicians and singers and take them off to the 'harmony' camps to have their minds wiped. Then, when they come out of the camps, they can't remember how to play or sing.

GirlFriendZ are the last band left, so MIB are desperate to catch them. If they do that, then that really *will* be the day music dies. But I'm never going to let that happen!

The Zargons

The Zargons are an alien race from the Andromeda galaxy. They have developed advanced technology that enables their starships to travel faster than the speed of light.

They are humanoid in appearance and, contrary to popular opinion, they do not possess tentacles (or tails!). However, in certain conditions, their eyes glow like cats' eyes.

They are on a mission to eradicate all forms of music from the universe. To this end, the Zargons build 'harmony' camps on the planets they invade. Anyone with musical talent is taken to the camps by Zargon agents of MIB (*Music Is Banned*), where they are subjected to a process known as 'mind wiping'. The mind-wipe has the effect of making the musician or singer forget how to play or sing. In street slang this process is known as 'soul stealing'.

The main feature of the 'harmony' camps are the giant incinerators where musical instruments are destroyed.

It is believed that the Zargons' hatred of music stems from the fact that music is the only thing that has the power to defeat them. (See article: *vampires*, *garlic*, *crosses*.)

Prologue

London, England. Saturday 2nd August 2025

'Thank you Wembley. It's been emotional.'

Kelly punched the air with her fist and 70,000 fans screamed back at her. Yaz, Olivia, Eve and Charlotte, the other members of *GirlFriendZ*, jumped up and down on the stage like hyperactive kangaroos. Waves of love washed over them from their fans. If they hadn't known they were the world's biggest band before this gig – they knew it now!

'Hey, listen to those guys,' yelled Charlotte.

'Yay, it's awesome,' Eve yelled back at her.

Olivia grinned like a cat with a bowl of double cream. 'It just doesn't get any better than this.'

'Yes it does,' said Yaz. 'This show's being beamed worldwide by satellite. Billions of people are going mad for us.'

* * * * * * *

Suddenly a huge shadow covered the stadium. The howling crowd fell silent. A giant starship hovered over Wembley.

At first people thought it was part of the show. But then a red laser light shot out from the ship and vapourised the Wembley

arch. A metallic voice rang out into the
stunned silence.

'People of Earth, go to your homes and
stay there. This is an order. Failure to obey
will be punishable by death. This planet is
now a province of the Zargon Empire.'

One
Buskers

The passengers on the tube train burst into applause as *GirlFriendZ*, the world's most popular band, took a bow. Then the doors slid open and Kelly, Eve, Yaz, Charlotte and Liv leapt out, sprinted across the platform and jumped onto a train going the other way.

As soon as they were safely on board they began to sing *Rock It Out*, their latest

download hit. The passengers roared their approval.

The five girls were taking a huge risk by singing in public. The Zargon invaders had banned all music and MIB agents worked tirelessly to stamp it out by mind-wiping singers and musicians. But *GirlFriendZ* were leading the fight back. Their latest plan to keep music alive was to go busking on the underground. They figured that by train-hopping they could reach a big audience, while staying one step ahead of any MIB soul-stealers. So far, their plan was working!

When the train pulled into the next station and the band was about to leave, a girl pushed a leaflet into Charlotte's hand. She beamed happily and said, 'Thanks, Charlotte, we can't wait to download *Sing a Song of Sixpence*. All of us fans just know it's going to be brilliant!'

Charlotte stared at the brightly-coloured piece of paper. Underneath an old publicity photo of *GirlFriendZ* were the words:

Calling all GirlFriendZ fans. MIB can't silence us. Download our new tune 'Sing a Song of Sixpence' on Friday 13th at Midnight. It's a killer track!

Charlotte stuffed the paper in her pocket and ran. But she knew something was very wrong. *GirlFriendZ* had no plans to release a new download – and certainly not one with the same name as the old nursery rhyme!

Two

Black Ops

When the girls arrived back at the dingy flat in the tower block where they were hiding out, Charlotte showed them the leaflet.

Kelly snatched it from her and waved it angrily. 'This is some kind of a scam. But who's behind it?'

'My guess is that it's MIB,' said Liv.

Charlotte shook her head. 'No way!
Those guys can't stand music. It scrambles
their brains like eggs in a microwave.'

Yaz looked thoughtful. 'Maybe it's an
MIB black ops trick,' she said. 'Those

sneaky freaks are always up to something nasty.'

Eve nodded. 'Yeah it could be them. The Zargons hate music, but they know nothing about it – otherwise they'd realise we'd rather be mind-wiped than sing an old nursery rhyme.'

'Huh, you speak for yourself,' said Charlotte indignantly.

'Hey, none of us want to be mind-wiped,' said Kelly. She frowned and tapped the leaflet with her finger. 'OK, we're agreed this is an MIB scam, but why do they want our fans to download a bogus track?'

The girls all shook their heads – they didn't have a clue.

Then Finn, the girls' road manager, spoke up. 'There's only one way to find out.'

The girls all stared at him expectantly.

'Someone has to infiltrate MIB headquarters and discover what game they're playing.' He paused and then added, 'But one thing for sure is that it won't be anything good!'

Three

Acting the Part

The girls glanced at each other. They all had the bitter taste of fear on their tongues. None of them wanted to be the one to try and sneak into MIB HQ.

Kelly swallowed audibly. 'So which one of us is going to volunteer?' she said.

There were no takers.

'Before we decide that,' said Finn hurriedly, 'we have to figure out how to beat the ID checker at the entrance to the building. Zargons have got that weird glow in their dark eyes, so it scans the pupils of everyone who enters MIB HQ to make sure they really are Zargons.'

The girls scratched their heads and wracked their brains to come up with a solution. Then Eve smiled and clicked her fingers.

'Hey, that's easy. We can use my special cat's eye contact lenses that I wore when we made our *I'm an Animal* video.' Then her face fell. 'So I guess that means *I'm* the one who gets to be the spy.'

Kelly shook her head. 'No way, Eve. The lenses may fool the Zargons, but not your trade-mark crazy hair!'

Eve tugged at her wild locks. 'I could shave my head,' she said.

Charlotte raised her eyebrows. 'Oh, like that won't make you stand out in the crowd!' she said sarcastically. 'No, Eve, I'll do it. I may not be the best singer in the band, but I am the best actress. Don't forget I was a child star in a TV soap before I joined *GirlFriendZ*, so playing the part of a Zargon is going to be a piece of cake!'

Eve sighed with relief and the other girls all gave Charlotte a hug. Despite what Charlotte said, they knew that what she was about to do was the most dangerous thing any of them could imagine.

Finn handed Charlotte an earring. 'Wear this, he said. 'It's got an app inside it that translates Zargon into English, so at least you'll know what they're saying.'

Then he reached out and solemnly shook her hand. 'Good luck, kid,' he said. 'You are going to need it!'

Four

Friday 13th

Charlotte strode up to the ID scanner. With a touch of skilfully applied make up she looked nothing like her normal self, but even so her mouth was dry and her stomach was knotted with nerves.

The machine shone a beam of light into her eyes and they glowed a nasty yellow colour. For a second the machine remained silent and Charlotte felt the panic rise up into her throat. Then its metallic voice said, 'You are cleared for entry.'

The doors to MIB HQ opened and Charlotte walked inside, ready to give the acting performance of her life.

She went over to the lifts and pressed the button. Two MIB agents walked up behind her. They were talking animatedly. 'This latest plan of ours is a masterstroke,' said one.

The other agent nodded. 'It is,' he agreed. 'When the stupid humans download *Sing a Song of Sixpence* on Friday the 13th, they will get far more than they bargained for.'

The first MIB agent made a noise like a rusty file scraping against metal. To her horror, Charlotte realised he was chuckling.

'Yes,' he said. 'Friday the 13ᵗʰ really *will* be an unlucky day for them. Instead of hearing that vile band *GirlFriendZ*, they will hear a Zargon mind-wipe hypno podcast. It will grip their weak little human brains and they will be powerless to prevent it from making them hate all kinds of music!'

Their words chilled Charlotte's blood.

Five

Lucky For Some

When the two agents left the lift, Charlotte followed them to their office. She glanced casually at them as she strolled past and made a note of the number they punched into the keypad on the door.

Charlotte hid in the toilet until everybody had left the building for the night. Then she crept back to the office and let herself in.

She hacked into the computer and saw a file named *Sixpence*.

'OK,' she muttered to herself, 'that must be the mind-wipe podcast.'

She was about to delete it and make her escape when she had an idea. She opened the folder, pointed her smartphone at the computer and pressed the data transfer app. Immediately, the mind-wipe podcast in the *Sixpence* folder was replaced with some brand new tracks that *GirlFriendZ* had recorded while in hiding.

Charlotte grinned. 'Yes, *GirlFriendZ* fans really *will* get something more than they bargained for when they download *Sing a Song of Sixpence*,' she murmured. 'But so will the Zargons!'

Suddenly she heard footsteps outside. Charlotte ducked down behind a desk as

the door opened and one of the MIB agents walked in!

'Now where did I leave my blasted comphone?' he muttered. 'It must be in here somewhere.'

Charlotte looked down and saw a small gadget lying on the floor right next to her. She guessed it must be the comphone. The MIB agent started to turn the office upside down, searching for his lost phone. Charlotte knew it was only a matter of time before he saw her.

She reached out to pick the comphone up, but her hands were sweating so much it slipped out of her grasp and skidded across the floor. It stopped right behind the agent. He stepped back and trod on it. A string of Zargon swear words exploded from his mouth.

Then the other agent poked his head round the door. 'That'll teach you to be more careful where you put your stuff,' he said. 'Now come on – this last lot of *GirlFriendZ* leaflets are not going to deliver themselves.'

Grumbling and swearing, the MIB agent stomped out of the office, slamming the door behind him.

Charlotte sighed with relief. She pulled out her phone and called Finn.

'Hey, Finn,' she said. 'I know people say it's only a silly superstition, but trust me, Friday the 13th is going to be a really unlucky day for the Zargons!'